P9-BBV-973

For Joe and Jerome, my own Arlo and Spot.
—B.D.

To my mother, for her love, kindness, and years of sacrifice.
A good friend and teacher whom our family would be lost without.
—D.S.

To all the little Spots in the wild, be fearless!
—M.E.N.

Printed in the United States of America
First Hardcover Edition, October 2015
1 3 5 7 9 10 8 6 4 2
FAC-03427-15240
ISBN 978-1-4231-8752-3
Library of Congress information available
Visit www.disneybooks.com

Disney · PIXAR

THE GOOD DINOSAUR

A Friend in the Wild

by Brandi Dougherty

illustrated by Denise Shimabukuro

and Maria Elena Naggi

Disney PRESS

Los Angeles • New York

Arlo has a friend in the wild: Spot!

Spot taught Arlo how to survive. Arlo showed Spot how to thrive.
They take good care of each other.

Making your way in the world? Here are some tips.

Build yourself a good, sturdy **shelter**.

Gather Food. Not only is it essential for survival; it's fairly easy once you get the hang of it.

Look for fresh water.

You'll be surprised by what you can find!

Stay alert in case of danger.
You never want to be caught off guard.

Be sure to **learn your plants.**

You'll be glad you did!

Along with the basics, like food, water, and shelter, always **have a friend** by your side.

When an obstacle gets in your way,

Work together to overcome it.

Get to know your friend by heart.

The more you know,
the better!

A friend can help you **weather the storm.**

Don't forget to **have fun**!

You never know who you might meet in the wild.

Be open to adventure . . .

. . . and wonder.

OW-OOOOOOOOOO!

If you're having trouble seeing in the dark,

Light your way.

OW-OOOOOOOOOOO!

Stick together!

Make sure you have a way
to find each other
in case you get lost.

At the end of a long day, find a comfy spot to curl up. A friend in the wild will help you **stay safe and warm.**

Good luck!